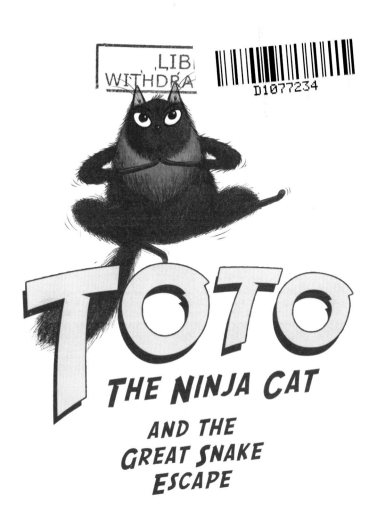

TOTO

THE NINJA CAT

AND THE
GREAT SNAKE
ESCAPE

DERMOT O'LEARY

ILLUSTRATED BY NICK EAST

HODDER CHILDREN'S BOOKS

First published in Great Britain in 2017 by Hodder and Stoughton

1 3 5 7 9 10 8 6 4 2

Text copyright © Dermot O'Leary, 2017
Illustrations copyright © Nick East, 2017
Inside back cover photograph by Ray Burmiston

A CIP catalogue record for this book
is available from the British Library.

ISBN 978 1 444 93945 3

Printed and bound in Great Britain by Clays Ltd, St Ives plc

The paper and board used in this book
are made from wood from responsible sources

MIX
Paper from
responsible sources
FSC® C104740

Hodder Children's Books
An imprint of
Hachette Children's Group
Part of Hodder and Stoughton
Carmelite House
50 Victoria Embankment
London EC4Y 0DZ

An Hachette UK Company
www.hachette.co.uk
www.hachettechildrens.co.uk

TO SILVER AND TOTO:

the most incredible, tough, loving
little Puglian *paisanos.*

And to all of you out there who also know
that your cat has a double life as a night-time ninja,
but keep it your secret.

CHAPTER 1

Toto was having the best dream of her life (featuring an enormous pepperoni pizza, a bucket of cheesy pasta and, to finish, her furry face buried in a massive tiramisu), when she found herself **RUDELY** transported back to a cold London night.

CRASH, BANG and, while we're at it, *WALLOP* doesn't even come close to the terrible noise that disturbed the silence on the otherwise sleepy street. It was the kind of night where you and I would be tucked up in bed with an extra blanket and a hot-water bottle. The kind of night where no one in their right mind would get out of bed until the lazy winter sun rises and makes it just about OK to face the new day.

And that's just for us humans. For cats? *FORGET ABOUT IT!* No cat would be seen dead getting out of a snuggly bed when it was this cold. They'd never be able to show their furry faces in polite cat society again. No. 'Best leave it to the foxes and the rats,' most cats would say. 'Let's get some shut-eye and I'll see you some time tomorrow about, oh, let's say, eleven-ish ...'

Which is why Toto was annoyed, tired and just a little bit scared when she heard the **ALMIGHTIEST DIN** coming from the bins outside.

Toto looked at her parents. *They'll sort this out, won't they?* she thought. They hadn't moved a muscle. They weren't even stirring.

'Honestly,' Toto muttered to herself, 'who are the cats and who are the humans here? *We're* supposed to be the ones who sleep all the time, and *you're* supposed to be the ones who get us food, pet us, lavish us with attention, groom us, open doors for us, turn on taps for us to drink water, massage our feet, and most importantly ...

GET UP WHEN THERE ARE SCARY NOISES OUTSIDE!

It's a fair deal ... but to recap: WE are supposed to be the sleepers!'

She looked over at her brother Silver, who, as his name suggests, had silver and white fur, with a big bushy tail and white paws.

Toto, on the other hand, was a big ball of black, grey and brown fur, especially with her winter coat on. She had a ruff around her neck, which made her look like a cat that wouldn't be out of place in Elizabethan England, as opposed to where she was really from – a place called Puglia, in the heel of Italy. She and Silver were stray cats and they had arrived in London only three weeks ago, after they were rescued by two kind humans, who they now called Mum and Dad. (Or, as Toto would say, Mamma and Papa.) The ones who currently lay snoring in their bed.

'Silver,' whispered Toto. '**SILVER!** Did you hear that? I think it came from outside, from the bins … **OUR BINS!**'

'I didn't hear a thing,' said Silver, yawning and stretching.

'Yes you did, you liar, that's why you're awake. Look, this is our house now – that means it's our turf! We have to go and investigate.'

'OK, well, maybe I did hear something, but it could be foxes!

YAWN

Have you seen the size of them? They're not like the countryside ones we're used to. These guys are mean. Terrifying! Let's just stay here and wait for it to die down.'

'YOU'RE SCARED!' said Toto.

'Well, er, no, it's just that it is a very cold night, plus the cat flap is such a pain to open, and ... Oh yes, all right, I admit it. I'm *a bit* scared. Look, Toto, we've been in this country for three weeks, we're just trying to fit in, it's cold, we're warm-blooded and Italian, and now I've been woken up by who-knows-what downstairs, and you're asking me to go and investigate. **WHY DON'T YOU GO?'**

'Silver, that could be a little tricky. I'm blind, remember?!' said Toto.

Toto had a point. She was as blind as a bat and had been since birth.

Actually, that's not *totally* true. Firstly, she'd already met the neighbourhood bat, Eric, and while she didn't get a chance to have a chat – something about 'insects to catch, no time to stop' – he certainly didn't *seem* blind. And secondly, well, she could see *something* ... Up very close her eyesight was just about OK, but from further away all she could see were light and dark shapes. She could recognise outlines of things (like Mamma and Papa), cats (like her brother), birds outside (they looked tasty!) and really anything that moved. But she always liked to have Silver by her side. Yes, he was a pain at times, teasing her, but like most big brothers he was fiercely loyal and loved his sister very much … not that he would EVER say that in public.

'Yes, sis,' replied Silver, 'I know you're blind, but you're also a ninja, remember?!'

Now, *he* had a point. Toto was in fact one of the most skilled ninja cats on earth, a member of a select elite club of cat ninjas, with skills she'd learnt as a kitten from her master in Italy, an old ship's cat called Ventura, who had in turn learnt from his master in Japan, who in turn could trace his ninja skills back hundreds of years … In other words, yes, Silver had a point. Toto could look after herself.

'Fine,' said Toto. 'Let's go down together. You for your eyes—'

'And charm,' Silver added.

'Yes, and charm,' said Toto, rolling her eyes, 'and me for—'

'Your deadly ninja skills,' Silver finished.

'Deal,' said Toto.

'*DEAL,*' said Silver.

Silver was right. Ninja or not, the cat flap was a nightmare to get through. Why didn't Mamma and Papa just leave the door open? Toto and Silver had grown up in an olive grove, so any door or cat-flap-based scenario was still a bit odd to them. But once they were out, it was simple enough – a short hop across the garden, over the wall, and they arrived at the front of the house where the bins were kept.

In the inky darkness, the moon lit up an enormous figure, twice the size of both of them. Its top half was hanging precariously over the bin while its, frankly, *shapely* bum and legs dangled in the night air.

'So,' Toto whispered, as they hid behind a car in the driveway, 'it's definitely not a fox.'

'**TOTO, YOU CAN'T SEE!** How can you be sure?' replied Silver.

'Don't be so rude. I can see shapes, images, lights, darks and these –' she pointed angrily to her ears and whiskers – 'aren't there just for show, you know! I can sense things. Besides, does it look like a fox to you?'

'Well, no,' said Silver. 'It's not exactly fox-like. But for the life of me I have no idea what it is. Too big to be rat, but surely far too fat to be a cat?'

As 'it' surfaced from the bin with bits of food all around its mouth, the mystery became clearer, but only a little.

The animal had light-brown fur and was dressed in a tweed jacket, with a pork-pie hat and a red cravat tied around its neck.

Toto and Silver looked at each other, confused. Was it a cat, after all? It had to be – just a very odd, enormous one. One thing was certain – it was making such a racket, it wasn't exactly trying to hide.

'I think it's one of us,' whispered Toto.

'Shame,' said Silver. 'I could have done with a rat sandwich as a midnight snack. Best thing about London – all the rats to eat.'

'Oh, rather!' muttered the creature to itself. 'Oh, this nosh is **EXTRAORDINARY** – top-drawer. This has to be one of my favourite bins in London. Lovely mackerel bone, nice bit of old paté, little morsel of brie ...'

Toto and Silver peeked around the car, then crouched back down, even more confused than before.

'What's he on about?' whispered Toto.

'Beats me,' said Silver. 'He's enjoying himself though.'

'But it's *our* bin,' said Toto. '*Our* front garden.'

'Do you really want to eat out of a bin?' said Silver. 'Toto, we're on easy street here – we get three meals a day, out of a tin. A TIN, Toto! We are pampered, worshipped, adored. Our buddies back in Italy would kill for this, and you're worried about ... a bin!'

'Well, fine, but he is on our turf, so let's go and check him out,' said Toto.

'Right behind you,' Silver said.

As far as silent and deadly stalking goes, Toto was an expert, even for a cat. Thanks to her ninja training she could move almost silently; thanks to her whiskers she always knew exactly where she was; and thanks to her exceptional hearing she could detect any movement in a kilometre radius.

She was so silent, she was practically invisible. Sadly, the same couldn't be said for her brother.

Toto was *about* to say, 'Listen, when we get over there, here's what we should do ...'

but she was interrupted by Silver tripping over a small shrub (*How was that possible?* she thought to herself. *It would have been easier NOT to trip up!*) and landing on Toto's back, sending them both sprawling at the feet of the mystery intruder.

'**AHHHH!**' the intruder yelled as he jumped two metres into the night sky. As he landed, an extraordinarily long, thin tail shot out from beneath his tweed jacket before disappearing again.

'Now, here's a thing,' said the creature, looking down at them. 'Two cowards creeping up on me to rob me while I enjoy supper from my own bin, hey? What have you got to say for yourselves?'

'**WELL, FIRSTLY, IT'S NOT YOUR BIN,**'

Toto said as she scrambled out from underneath her brother. 'Secondly, we've just moved here from Italy, but this is OUR front garden, and we don't take too kindly to other cats on our turf. Right, Silver? Silver?' She turned around to see her brother tucking into a half-empty yoghurt pot that had been spilt in all the commotion. 'Silver!'

'Oh, absolutely, what she said. *Mamma mia, I love yoghurt*,' he added to no one in particular, his head now buried in the pot.

'Ah right, of course!' the intruder spluttered, looking a bit shifty. 'As you can see, I *am* a cat, and I had no idea that other cats had moved in here, so I suppose I just staked a claim to this bin. No harm done. Like you said, we're all cats. Huzzah for cats! Now, I take it the young man with his face stuck in a pot is Silver, which makes you … ?'

'Toto,' she answered, a little surprised by how charming this odd-looking cat was. 'And you are?'

SLURP

'Young lady and sir, welcome, and allow me to introduce myself. You have the pleasure of making the acquaintance of Alexandre Rattinoff the Thirty-third, but you fine people can address me as all my dear friends do ... My name is Catface.'

'CATFACE?' Toto and Silver said together.

'Yes.'

'You're a cat. **CALLED CATFACE?'**

'Yes.'

'I hope you don't think we're being rude,' said Toto, 'but that's a strange name. Your *face* obviously looks like a *cat*, because ... you *are* a cat.'

'Ah, well, you are recent arrivals here in London, but rest assured, it's very common, in fact all the rage in polite feline society, to call your kitten Catface. A fine name,' he said, pulling at his cravat and looking *very* nervous.

'If you say so,' Toto muttered to Silver.

'Anyway, now that we've made each other's acquaintance – nay, *friendship* – let me just enjoy the last of this delicious brie. *AH, STINKY ...*'

Toto and Silver looked at each other and shrugged.

'Lovely. So, my young friends,' said Catface, licking the last of the cheese from his chops, 'you've just moved here. What do you make of your new hometown? Have you seen the Crown Jewels? Buckingham Palace? Number 10 Downing Street? London Zoo? Some fantastic beasts to see there, although many are rather partial to a small feline snack such as ourselves, so probably best avoided. Well, come on, I can't wait to hear your first impressions.'

Toto and Silver looked at him blankly.

'What is it?' said Catface.

'We have no idea what you're talking about,' said Silver.

Catface looked aghast. 'You haven't been given a tour? By anyone?'

'No, we've just been playing, chilling, watching TV. Our parents watch a lot of nature programmes. Some of the cats they have on there! Massive!' said Silver.

'Now, this really is a **DISGRACE!**' said

Catface. 'It is, however, your lucky night, as I am registered with the guild of cat tourist guides. Why, only last week I gave a guided tour to the Belgian foreign minister's cat, Adelia, a lovely Russian Blue. And tonight, after that delicious meal from your bin, I am indebted to you, so I am free for the next few hours to show you this glorious city of ours. What say you?'

'Well, it *is* really cold, and we might get in trouble—' Silver began.

'We'd love to,' interrupted Toto. 'Where do we begin?'

'We begin, of course, with a journey to central London,' said Catface.

'Right. And how will we get there?' Toto said, as they headed off down the street.

'Like any self-respecting Londoner, dear girl,' replied Catface.

'WE'LL TAKE THE TUBE!'

CHAPTER 2

Toto and Silver weren't entirely sure what the Tube was, where it was and what it did, so they were a little nervous as they followed Catface away from the safety and comfort of their new home.

'So, my little mites, you said you were from Italy. Where exactly, and how in the world did you find yourselves in Camden Town?' Catface asked.

'It's been a pretty strange few weeks to be honest,' said Silver. 'We're from Puglia, in the heel of the boot of Italy. We were born in an olive grove and we lived in the roots of a massive, gnarled old olive tree. The grove  was beautiful, and huge – the trees went on as far as we could see, which wasn't that far in Toto's case.'

'Hmm, the old eyesight a little squiffy, is it?' said Catface. 'Can't say you're on your own there, Toto. I think I'm going to need some reading glasses myself soon ... Go on.'

'Well,' said Toto, 'we never really knew our cat mamma and papa – they moved on when we were little. It's the way of the world for cats where we're from. But they left us with some food and we learnt skills to fend for ourselves.'

'It was hard, but we had each other,' Silver continued. 'The weather was great, we had lots of olives to eat, and there were small green lizards everywhere. Though they'd always give you a sob story about a wife and eggs back home, so I let most of them go. There were lots of tasty rats though – we *LOVED* eating them.'

Catface shuddered.

'Are you OK?' asked Silver.

'Fine, fine, just a little chilly,' said Catface hastily. 'So, how did you end up here?'

Toto picked up the story. 'Well, to be honest, we were a bit lonely. It's not nice being a stray. The grove was next to a house, and one day our new mamma and papa came to visit. They found us in a tree after a big storm, gave us lots of cuddles and food, and let us sleep inside! Next thing we knew we were on this thing called an aeroplane – no idea how it works, but it fires you into the sky – and here we are, in London.'

'Oh, and did we mention that Toto is a nin—' Silver broke off as Toto shot him a look.

'A what?' asked Catface.

'A NIGHT OWL!' replied Toto. 'I just love the night.'

'Well, that is excellent news,' said Catface, 'as we have a wonderful night ahead of us.'

They rounded a corner on to Camden High Street, which was deserted apart from a couple of guys with red spiky hair who didn't pay any attention to three cats padding by. Bits of rubbish swirled in the cold wind, and the yellow street lights illuminated the famous red, white and blue of the Tube station.

Catface noticed the two cats looking uncertain. 'Oh, don't you worry, my friends, it's perfectly safe. It'll be the ride of your lives!'

Not entirely convinced, the cats followed him across the empty road.

'Listen,' whispered Silver to Toto, 'why did you stop me from telling Catface that you're a ninja? If I had your skills I'd be meowing from the rooftops about them.'

'Silver, being a ninj— a *you-know-what* – isn't like supporting a football team. I'm an elite warrior with a unique set of skills, ready to be called upon at any time by one of my kind! I can't just tell everyone we meet and let the cat out of the bag ... Excuse the pun.'

'Eggy,' said Silver. 'Righty-ho, sorry. I'm just proud of you and, you know, I want us to make a good impression round here.'

'I get it,' said Toto. 'Let's just keep it on the down-low at the mo.'

'*On the down-low*,' laughed Silver. 'Check you out with your new London lingo!'

'I saw it on TV, all right!' Toto replied, and gave her brother an affectionate bite on the ear as they ran to catch up with Catface.

Go *on the Tube* is what Londoners do. What they also do – thankfully for London's furry animal population – is *never look up*. They are too busy staring at their feet or at their phones.

Which is a shame, because if they did look up, they would see a whole army of furry hitch-hikers using their public transport system.

'Oh no, we don't go through that entrance,' said Catface, walking straight past the Camden Town Tube station sign. 'That's for humans, with their queuing and moaning and what have you. *VIP ALL THE WAY FOR US, MY FURRY FRIENDS!'*

On a side street round the corner, they came to an old rusty door at cat-height that most humans wouldn't ever notice. Catface pulled at a small brass doorknob which opened on to an iron spiral staircase descending as far as the eye could see. All sorts of animals were going up and down the stairs, and unlike their fellow human travellers they were very, very talkative.

'What is all this?' Silver asked, his eyes wide.

'This, my friends, is how all animals, even the birds if they are feeling lazy, travel around London ... twenty-four hours a day. **ALL ABOARD!'**

At the foot of the stairs they emerged into a beautiful high-ceilinged ticket hall, tiled in black and white and lit by two massive chandeliers, which in turn led to a platform.

Catface pointed out the humans rushing about on their own platform below, which they could see through air vents in the floor.

The animals' platform was almost identical, with waiting benches and twinkling lights, and even adverts on the walls for dog food, budgie trill and catnip.

There must have been every kind of animal on the platform, all patiently waiting for the next train. Dogs, cats, ferrets, hedgehogs, parakeets, pigeons, you name it ... apart from rats. Silver and Toto were amazed that no one was attacking, growling or even hissing at each other.

Before the cats could ask why, Catface piped up. '*BEHOLD, THE ANIMAL TUBE!* It's a wonderful institution, with strict rules.

Everyone here is of the understanding that on the Tube we live and let live, no attacks allowed.' He beamed. 'The only exception being mice and rats, who have to travel on the underside of the train. We tried to integrate a while back, but cats and rats on the same platform didn't exactly ... er ... *work*, if you catch my drift. Ah, here we go.'

A clunky train pulled into the station to pick up the late-night workers and party-going humans down below.

'We sit on the roof?!' asked Toto, starting to feel just a little scared. On top of the human train was a carriage almost identical to the one below, although this one had no roof of its own.

'Of course!' said Catface. 'And I see we have a front-row seat. Hold on tight, my Italian friends, you are going to love this.'

As the train pulled away and picked up speed, it entered the tunnel with just centimetres to spare above their heads.

'AAAHH, THIS IS INCREDIBLE!' yelled Toto and Silver, feeling the air *whoosh* through their whiskers.

'The only way to travel, my friends! Just

you wait for our exciting first stop!' said Catface, as they disappeared into the darkness.

And so, over the next few hours, Catface treated the cats to a whistle-stop tour of every great sight London had to offer, with the most knowledgeable and best-loved guide. One thing was certain, even in a city this big, everybody knew Catface.

At St Paul's Cathedral, the bats in the belfry swooped down to say hello.

At the Tower of London, the ravens had saved him some beef to eat, which the cats tucked into.

At Buckingham Palace, they woke up the corgis for a cup of tea and toast.

At the Shard, the seagulls picked them up and flew them to the top of the highest building in London, where they saw just how big the city was for the first time. The seagulls had even saved them some pizza they'd scavenged, which made Silver very happy.

By two a.m. the cats were worn out, and very full! And they'd made a lot of new friends.

'Anyone who's a friend of Catface is a friend of ours,' squawked Mary, the head gull.

But as tired and full as the cats were, there was one last stop before home. At a very important place ...

CHAPTER 3

'I didn't know London was so big!' said Toto, as they ambled down a side street near Whitehall, just by the Houses of Parliament.

'My dear,' replied Catface, 'we've barely scratched the surface. We'll have to make this a regular outing. It would be my pleasure.'

As they turned into an otherwise quiet street, Silver noticed a lot of parked cars and men in uniform milling around.

'Where are we now, Catface?' he asked. 'This all looks pretty important.'

'Indeed,' said Catface. 'This is 10 Downing Street, the home of the human Prime Minister – the person in charge of the whole country! Before I take you home I want to introduce you to a dear friend of mine. Now, hop up on that ledge so none of these fine police officers see us. They get a bit funny about loads of cats around here.'

The narrow ledge was about two floors up and ran the length of the houses in the street. For humans it would have been a big climb and a big drop – for cats it was a piece of cake. They walked along it till they were almost over the door of 10 Downing Street itself. Toto and Silver were working out how to jump down, when ahead of them Catface suddenly lost his footing and slipped, hurtling towards the ground.

'Toto!' Silver cried. 'Now would be a very good time to show off your ninj—'
But his sister had already disappeared into the darkness below.

Toto knew that a) she was in a really bad mood with her brother for mentioning the NINJ word and b) she'd better hurry, as Catface was about to get squished. Luckily (although for a ninja, luck wasn't too necessary), she could just make out his shape, and more importantly, she could hear the almighty scream coming from his mouth.

Toto caught up with Catface a metre or so off the ground and positioned her body so that she'd take the brunt of the fall.

AAAAAAAAAAAAAAAAAAAAAGGGGHH

Then, just as they were about to hit the ground, and the thought of Catface landing on her wasn't exactly top of Toto's wish list, she effortlessly pushed him off. He landed safely in a pile of leaves, while she landed nimbly on her feet.

'Well, that was rather **SPECTACULAR**,' said a white and grey tabby cat, who was leaning against the door of Number 10, a martini glass full of milk in his paw and a bowler hat at a jaunty angle on his head. 'Catface, my dear friend, you do know how to make an entrance!'

Catface brushed himself down and tried to regain some composure. 'Just a slip, my good chum. Happens all the ... er ... time.'

'Hmm, just as well this young lady was on hand to save the day, hey? So, aren't you going to introduce us?' said the tabby cat.

'Of course! It's the reason we're here!' replied Catface. 'Allow me to present two young friends of mine, recently moved here from Puglia in Italy, from smashing families

– local land owners and olive barons, no less. This is Toto and her brother, Silver.'

Silver had climbed down from the ledge and joined his sister. 'How do you do,' they both said, as if they were meeting royalty.

'A pleasure to meet you,' said the tabby cat, 'and bravo for saving our friend here. I thought he was a goner for a second. I served in the Queen's Cat Regiment as a young nipper. Tell me, young lady, with moves like that, are you ex-Italian special forces? I know a couple of Bengals who served there.'

Toto glared at Silver, as if to say, *Don't say a word!*

'No,' she said, 'those are just some tricks I picked up in the olive groves back home. Er … we didn't catch your name?'

'So sorry, where are my manners?' Catface said. 'Toto, Silver, allow me to introduce Chief Mouser, Head of Guest Liaison, Head of Feline Security, and Head of Quality Control for All Antique Furniture of a Napping Standard ... this is **LARRY THE CAT**.'

Toto and Silver bowed solemnly. It made them feel rather silly, but they could tell Larry was an important cat, and it seemed like the right thing to do, somehow.

'The pleasure is all mine,' said Larry. 'Oh, don't bow – a shake of the paw is quite enough. So Catface is showing you around, is he? Welcome to 10 Downing Street. Wonderful house. Almost four

hundred years old – it has a lot of stories to tell.'

'So, Larry, what's the news?' asked Catface. It was clear they were old friends.

'Well, it's been rather busy. We had the Belgian party in last week, which you helped us out with. Thank you for that – they loved the tour. We've got the Russian cats coming on a diplomatic trip next month, and to top it off there were a couple of parakeets flying over about half an hour ago, making the most **AWFUL RACKET**. I could barely understand them – something about a commotion up in Regent's Park. I say, isn't that your neck of the woods?'

'It is indeed, but I'm sure it's nothing,' said Catface. 'Parakeets are a hysterical bunch.

Still, I'd best check it out and get these two back to their humans.'

'Well, it's a pleasure to meet you, Toto and Silver. Make sure you drop by again sometime. I need to learn that move – very impressive. Now, if you'll excuse me, I have some night rounds to make. Good evening.'

At that, Larry tipped his pristine bowler hat and padded off up the street.

'Larry is quite possibly the coolest, most debonair cat in town, and certainly the most important,' said Catface, watching him go. 'Right, you two, let's get you home. Quite enough excitement for one night. And, Toto, thank you! I don't know where you learnt that move, but I do think you saved my bacon. Silver, what are you staring at?'

Silver was looking intently down a drain at the side of the street. 'What's down here?' he asked. 'I can hear noises. Is it rats? Is it? Can we go down? I haven't caught a rat in ages! Come on, let's do it! Toto? Catface?'

Catface looked pale. 'Oh no – no rats down there,' he spluttered, 'not with all the cats round here. No rat in their right mind would risk it. That's the sewer. You probably just heard the water whooshing and creaking through the tunnels. Yes, that's what it is, simple as that. Come on,' he said, walking off in the direction of the Tube.

'Good *you-know-what* work back there, sis,' Silver said, once Catface was out of earshot. 'But did you think it was a bit weird for a cat to fall like that? I mean, you and I could make that jump easily. Plus, it was definitely rats I heard down that drain, I swear it. Catface is a lovely guy, but you have to admit, he is a little weird.'

'I'll give you that,' Toto said. 'He's an odd fish all right, but we're new in town, so maybe *we're* the odd ones? Come on, let's catch up.'

As the cats stepped off the Tube at Camden Town, not far from Regent's Park, it was clear that the parakeets had good reason to be hysterical. What had been a sleepy, tranquil night was now pandemonium. There were animals everywhere! The local dogs were barking (which in animal language is just shouting the same thing over and over again) and trying to get out of their gardens; the neighbourhood cats were hanging around the street corners, chatting loudly and looking moody. Birds of all sorts – blackbirds, pigeons, robins, tits – were swooping through the sky, making more noise than the rest of the animals put together. Even a couple of hedgehogs had emerged from a nearby bush, looking a bit sleepy and confused.

CAMDEN WAS IN ANIMAL CHAOS!

'Robert, what on earth is happening?' Catface asked a passing parakeet.

'You sure you want to know?' the bird replied, perching on top of a gate. 'It's the zoo. We flew over there about an hour ago, and the whole place is in uproar ... **BRIAN HAS ESCAPED!**'

CHAPTER 4

'BRIAN? ESCAPED? **BRIAN?** HOW CAN THIS BE? IT'S IMPOSSIBLE!' ranted Catface, his face sheet-white.

Toto and Silver looked at each other blankly. *Brian?*

'This is a disaster! We'll have to evacuate the whole of Camden now!' Catface continued. 'Thank you, Robert. Best of luck, eh. Are you heading out of town?'

'Don't worry about me,' chirped Robert. 'I've got these bad boys,' he said, flapping his wings. 'I can fly – Brian can't. It's you guys who need to worry – he'll be coming this way for sure. I'm off to squawk at more animals!'

'This is bad, kids, as bad as it gets,' said Catface. 'We are in deep doo-doo.'

Silver fell about laughing. 'Deep doo-doo! Brilliant. Toto, he said *DOO-DOO!*'

'My friends, you don't understand,' said Catface. 'We *have* to get you two safely home. Then I must be on my way, back to my family to warn them, and then I think I might make for the country ... high ground – Scotland, perhaps. I've got more family there. I can get the morning train and be there by lunchtime ...'

'I'm sorry,' said Toto, 'but **WHO IS BRIAN?** And why is everyone so scared of someone called ... *Brian*?'

'Listen very carefully,' said Catface. 'You have no idea what Brian is capable of. He's clever, he's silent, and he is almost impossible for humans to catch. Brian is the stuff of legend, a ghost story that mummy animals tell their kids to make them behave. *"If you don't eat all your dinner, Brian will come and gobble you up."* Only it's not a made-up story, it's true! If he comes this way, which he will, as there are so many of us to … *gobble* … we're all doomed. We have to get you inside.'

'But what *is* Brian?' asked Toto.

'Brian,' sighed Catface, 'is a snake. And no ordinary snake … He is the famous King Cobra of London Zoo, one of the deadliest snakes in the world. Everyone has feared this day from the moment he was given a home there. Now that he has escaped, he will eat whatever he finds: birds, snakes, you, me. He will then try to mate and have babies—'

'UGH, GROSS!' exclaimed Silver.

'Thanks for that,' continued Catface. 'If he finds a lady cobra, and there are many in captivity around London, they will have forty or fifty babies, and do you know who *they* will eat? **ALL OF US**.'

'But ... he's called *Brian*. He doesn't sound *that* scary,' said Silver.

'I know,' replied Catface. 'It's a ridiculous name. I'm sure it was given to him to make him sound a bit cuddly and friendly, two things he absolutely isn't. Now, back to your house, you two, and don't come out again until he is caught.'

'You said he's impossible for humans to catch. Why don't we have a go?' asked Toto.

'Have you taken leave of your senses?' asked Catface. 'He's one of the most dangerous animals on the planet, and you want to go off on some adventure to find him? And just suppose we do track him down, what then? I can't fight him – no one can. We have to get to safety *now*.'

They trudged back to the house where they had started their night-time adventure only a few hours before. Catface was about to help them over the gate, when Toto turned around, a steely look in her eye.

'Listen,' said Toto. 'This is your home, right? If you run now, you'll never come back. We've just got here, and we love it already. Yes, it's a bit cold, and your pasta is nowhere near as good as ours, but look at this street. All the animals live happily alongside each other. This is our home and I for one want to fight for it. So I'm not running away—'

'Sis, you can't run away,' Silver interrupted. 'You can't see where you're going.'

'Not helpful,' replied Toto. 'But yes, I wouldn't actually be able to see exactly where I was going, thank you, Silver.'

'You're welcome,' he said.

'So, what's it to be, Catface? Will you help us, and will you let us help you?'

Catface sighed, and smiled at the two little cats. 'Look, I'm a coward. I don't like fighting, and there is no way – **NO WAY** – we can defeat the awesome power of Brian. But if you insist on trying to capture him, then ... oh, I can't believe I'm saying this ... then I'll help. We'll have to start at the zoo to find out where he's headed. Oh my, we're all going to get eaten!'

'Keep it light, Catface,' said Silver. 'So, you're in?'

'I'm in,' said Catface.

'Good,' said Silver. 'Because we have no idea where the zoo is.'

Catface, of course, knew exactly where to go.

'Listen, you two,' he said, as they scampered down the moonlit street in the direction of Regent's Park, 'if we are going to the zoo, which I remind you is a BAD IDEA, it's very important that you stick with me, otherwise you might find yourself in the wrong animal enclosure, and that would be, well, BAD. We'll squeeze through the aviary, over the bridge, through the warthog enclosure, under the tunnel, turn right next to the aquarium—'

'The aquarium!' interrupted Silver. '*All right!* Let's eat!'

'Focus, Silver,' said Catface.
'Next to the aquarium,' he continued, 'we'll find the reptile house ...'

As they slipped under the zoo gates,
Toto could hear an almighty din.

All the animals, from the aardvarks to the zebras, were awake, all scared and all chattering away. That was *a lot* of animals, making *a lot* of noise.

'Right, this is it,' said Catface. 'I'll go and see if any of the reptiles know where Brian was heading when he escaped. Now, stay here and DO NOT go into any animal pens. They might look cute and furry, but this place is crawling with creatures who would eat you two without a second thought. So sit tight and don't meow a word until I get back, OK?'

'OK,' agreed Silver and Toto.

Catface disappeared inside the reptile house.

'Really?' said Silver. 'There are animals

from all over the world in this zoo – we might even be related to some of them – and he doesn't expect us to explore? You stay here if you want to – I'm off for a wander. **BESIDES, I CAN SMELL ICE CREAM.**'

Before Toto could argue, Silver was gone. She didn't know what to do. Follow her brother? Or wait for Catface? Before she could make up her mind, she heard the big wooden doors of the reptile house squeak open.

'You do *not* want to venture in there, my young ones,' said Catface. 'I think we look rather a lot like lunch to most of those chaps. Still, I've just spoken to a charming African bullfrog called Adam. Do you want the good news or the bad news?'

'I think we need some good news,' said Toto.

'Right you are. The good news is, Adam knows where Brian went.'

'And the bad news?'

'Brian was last seen heading towards the tiger enclosure.'

Toto didn't get it. How was this bad news? She was vaguely aware of what tigers were from the nature documentaries Silver loved so much, and she knew they were related to her. Just big cats. All they had to do was go and ask them, and they'd be one step closer to capturing Brian and saving London's wildlife.

'So, let's go to the tiger enclosure,' she said.

'That's the problem, Toto. I know most animals worth knowing in the whole of London, from the queen's corgis to the water voles of Barnes, from the peregrine falcons of Regent's Park to the sewer rats of Bermondsey, and even *I* wouldn't go anywhere near the tiger enclosure.

Tigers are animal royalty – have been for thousands of years. They're the top dogs – sorry, *cats* – and everyone is terrified of them. They eat whatever they want, no questions asked. One of my oldest friends, a pigeon called Carruthers, accidently landed in their pad last year. They only found two feathers to take back to his wife! Anyone who goes in there isn't coming out again, especially little blind cats from Italy ... Hang on, where's Silver?'

'He went for a wander,' replied Toto.

Catface looked horrified.

'Don't blame me,' Toto said. 'He's easily distracted, plus I think he smelt ice cream and he's a sucker for dairy. Look, we have to go and see the tigers. If we don't find

Brian, we'll all have to leave London – *not* an option – or be trapped inside our houses – *not* an option. You said it yourself – humans will never capture him. **THIS IS DOWN TO US!**'

Catface put a paw to his head. 'I do believe that you might just get me eaten, but I suppose we're too far in to turn back now. When word gets out that three furry critters are wandering around the zoo in the middle of the night – and trust me, it will – we'll be best off sticking together. So here's what I suggest: **LET'S GET YOUR BROTHER, NOT GET EATEN BY TIGERS AND GET OUT OF HERE WITH THE INFORMATION WE NEED AS QUICKLY AS POSSIBLE. FOLLOW ME!**'

Toto took a deep breath and padded after Catface as quietly as she could, heading deeper into the dimly lit zoo ...

CHAPTER 5

There were no street lamps in the zoo, so only the moon and stars lit up the cold night sky. The cats stuck to the shadows as they tiptoed past the African Bird Safari and the Gorilla Kingdom. Toto didn't fancy coming face-to-face with a huge silverback gorilla, even though Catface had assured her *they* actually posed no danger to a little Italian cat.

Better safe than sorry, thought Toto, as they skirted round the bend.

Then, looming out of the darkness, there it was: the entrance to Tiger Territory, marked by a wooden arch emblazoned with a picture of a tiger. Its hard stare seemed to be looking right at them.

'Here we are,' said Catface in a small voice. 'Let's do this. Then we can find Silver and get out of here.'

'Catface ... um ... *how* exactly should we do this?' Toto asked.

'Well,' said Catface, 'if by some miracle we don't get torn to shreds in the next thirty seconds, I suggest we show respect by making sure we're lower than them. And bow. They like bowing.'

'That shouldn't be too hard,' Toto replied as she jumped up on to the roof of the enclosure. 'They're going to be quite a lot bigger than us!'

Catface was struggling to jump high enough.

He's really bad at jumping for a cat,

thought Toto, *but he did have that big meal out of our bins earlier, plus all the food on our tour of London. Perhaps he's still a bit full?*

Eventually Catface made it on to the roof, then they both jumped down as silently as possible into the long grass and started walking slowly through the undergrowth.

After a minute or two they heard something – faint at first, but getting louder as they drew closer.

'Strange,' whispered Catface. 'Doesn't sound like a tiger.'

'That's because it isn't. *IT'S SILVER!*' Toto set off at a run through the undergrowth until she reached a clearing. She could just about make out Silver, clinging to the top of a giant pole.

'What are you doing up there? Get down now!' Toto hissed. 'Have you any idea how dangerous this is? Don't you know where you are?'

'Yes, thanks for stating the obvious, sis,' Silver called down. 'I'm really sorry – I just saw the raw meat up here and went for it. I didn't know it belonged to ... you know ... *them*.' He gestured behind Toto and Catface with his paw.

They both turned, knowing full well what was behind them, but praying that Silver might just be mistaken ...

Keep cool, Toto told herself. *You're a ninja, remember.*

Silver wasn't mistaken. Hungry? *Yes.* Greedy? *A bit.* Foolish? *Definitely.* But there was nothing wrong with Silver's eyesight.

Toto could make out two enormous shadows in the moonlight, stalking slowly and deliberately towards them. The tigers broke through the long grass and stood majestically before them, two sets of bright fiery eyes shining in the darkness.

'Er, now might be a good time to bow,' said Catface.

Toto swept one paw and stooped low, as if she was bowing in front of the queen.

'Let me handle this, little one.' Catface cleared his throat, took off his hat and made

a grand gesture as he bowed. 'All hail the king and queen of London Zoo. We come here to beg an audience and ask for your help to find Brian, the escaped King Cobra, who threatens all animals in London. We believe he came this way, and wanted to enquire if Your Highnesses are aware of his whereabouts on this very night of which I speak. *Ahem*.'

The tigers said nothing. They just stared.

'Do you think it's working?' whispered Catface.

'I'd like to say yes ... but right now I'm sort of thinking *no*,' replied Toto.

'Hmm. Tough gig, this. I say, do you know any tricks?'

Before Toto could answer, the larger of the two tigers spoke up in a low, commanding growl.

'**SMALL INSIGNIFICANT FELINES!** You dare to come into our home, to steal our food, uninvited. Animals have been torn apart for less!'

Toto and Catface looked up at Silver.

'Er, how do you do?' Silver began. 'Yeah, that was me I guess – sorry. I just saw this big slab of meat on top of this pole – what is it, by the way? Deer? It's *delicious* – and I went for it. Didn't know whose it was. Any chance you could let me off with a stern warning?'

'And WHAT,' bellowed the other tiger, 'makes you think that we, Jae Jae and Melati, should care about you and your kind? Brian the King Cobra always shows us respect, and passed through here earlier with our blessing. The animals of the zoo are our priority, not the *common folk* that live outside.'

'Now, look here,' Catface said furiously, taking a step towards the enormous cats. 'I know you are the king and queen of the zoo and what have you, but let me tell you, there are some smashing animals out there, and I for one will not stand by and let them get eaten by Brian and, heaven forbid, Brian's future kids ...'

Toto and Silver looked at each other. Had Catface gone mad? They were doomed!

The tigers said nothing for a minute, just stared.

I do wish they'd stop doing that, thought Toto.

Then the tigers nodded slightly to each other and slowly started to pace around the cats in a circle.

'We appreciate your bravery tonight, but we're afraid we can't help you,' said Melati, the smaller of the two. 'And I'm even more afraid to say that *we can't let you leave.*'

'It's so rare that we get the sport of *moving prey*,' growled Jae Jae. 'And besides, we have our reputation to consider. If we let you go now, we'd never live it down. What if those Asiatic lions got wind of it? *You must all die tonight.*'

'Oh dear,' whimpered Catface. 'That didn't *exactly* have the desired effect, did it?'

Toto knew what she had to do. Yes, the tigers were fast and powerful, but they were also large, and that meant she had two big targets to aim for. But first she had to get Catface out of harm's way.

Remembering her training and clearing her mind, she drew a breath very slowly, exhaled, then moved fast. Before the tigers knew what was happening, she'd picked Catface up by her teeth. She bounced – once, twice – off the trees, gaining height, then dropped him next to Silver at the top of the pole.

'You'll be safe here for now, so long as I keep them occupied,' Toto said.

Before Catface had the chance to ask, *Are you out of your mind?*, Toto had leapt off the pole, back into the darkness.

'Go get 'em, sis,' said Silver, grinning. 'Just watch this,' he said to Catface.

Toto knew the tigers were down there somewhere, but when she hit the ground she couldn't see any sign of them.

'Impressive, little one,' she heard one of them say through the long grass. 'But your efforts will be in vain. We are too big, and too powerful.'

Luckily, when you're a blind ninja cat, and someone you're about to fight uses words like **BIG** and **POWERFUL** to describe themselves, it also means that they're proud – and their pride means that they think they can't be beaten ... **BIG MISTAKE!**

As one of the tigers charged out of the undergrowth, Toto could sense exactly where the danger was coming from. She crouched with her back to a tree and, just as the tiger's massive jaws were about to close around her, she somersaulted into the air and on to a low branch.

MEEUW

Melati crashed helplessly into the tree below Toto, knocking herself clean out.

One down, one to go, thought Toto, as she lowered herself to the ground.

Jae Jae's shadow emerged from the undergrowth. 'Very good, young lady – you *are* fast. But how will you fare in one-to-one combat? There's nowhere to run and nowhere to hide ...'

No, thought Toto, *but there are a lot of places to leap.*

Just as the larger tiger went for her, she sprang off the ground and on to another branch. Jae Jae snarled and reached up, but once more Toto was too fast. She knew how she could beat him. Every time he swiped at her with his enormous claw, which could have cut her in two, Toto heard him just in time to jump out of the way.

'Argh, come here, you little furball! I'll tear you limb from limb!' Jae Jae snarled.

Toto could tell the tiger was getting tired and frustrated. She knew her chance was coming.

As the tiger overreached with another tired swipe, she sensed a gap in his defences, and launched herself at his big pink nose with all her strength and speed, digging her claws in. 'OOOWWWWW, that's not fair!' whined the tiger, clutching his nose.

SOB

'OK, OK – you win. *OWWW, IT REALLY HURTS!* I hope the zoo keeper has some cream to put on it.'

Toto was stunned. Jae Jae had turned into a sulky kitten! 'So ... er ... you give in?' she said.

'Yes, of course! I've never actually been scratched before! Why did you have to be so nasty?'

'Well, maybe because you were trying to eat me!' said Toto.

'I'll tell you what you want to know if you promise not to scratch me again,' said Jae Jae.

'OK with me!' said Toto.

Jae Jae went over to Melati just as she was shaking her head and coming to. Both tigers turned to Toto, started making the strangest noise and rolled on to their backs.

'What are they doing?' whispered Toto.

Catface smiled as he climbed down from the pole with Silver. 'I do believe they are *chuffing*. It sounds almost like a snort, and is what tigers do when they want to purr like you – I mean, *like us*. I think, my friend, that they want their tummies tickled.'

The cats looked at each other and shrugged. 'It beats getting torn limb from limb,' said Silver. 'And they *are* royalty.'

Cautiously, Toto, Silver and Catface made their way over to the tigers. They began rubbing their bellies, and unbelievably the tigers loved it.

'Oh yes, lovely … Left a bit, right a bit …

Ahhh, just right!' purred Jae Jae.

'Well then,' said Catface, after about five minutes of tickling, 'this is getting a tad awkward now, so if you could just tell us where Brian was going, we'd best be on our way.'

'Oh, do you have to go? Just one last scratch? OK, well ... Brian said he was heading to the sewers, near the canal,' said Jae Jae. 'He said he had some business down there.'

'Oh dear!' said Catface, looking pale. It was obviously not what he wanted to hear. **'THERE'S NOT A MINUTE TO LOSE!'**

The cats started to leave, but the tigers stopped them.

'We're sorry,' Jae Jae said to Toto. 'You may

be a commoner, but you truly are a warrior, and you may pass this way whenever you choose.'

'Thank you,' said Toto. 'Just one thing though: please try to remember that you should care about *all* the animals, rare or common.'

'You're right, of course, we'll try. Er, by the way, we'd really appreciate it if, you know, you didn't mention this to anyone. It's just that we've got a fearsome reputation to live up to, and this "losing a fight to a small cat" thing might not go down too well. Deal?'

'Deal,' said Toto.

'Yeah, deal,' said Silver. 'But I'm taking this bit of deer with me.'

As the three cats padded off, the tigers

looked at each other in disbelief.

'Who *was* that?' said Jae Jae.

'Her name is Toto,' Silver turned and called back. 'She's my sister, she's blind, **AND SHE'S THE INCREDIBLE NINJA CAT OF CAMDEN TOWN**. And don't you forget it!'

Toto looked at her brother and smiled. She'd never admit it, but she kind of liked the sound of that.

And so Toto, Silver and Catface strutted out of the zoo, towards the sewers, on the trail of the deadliest snake in the world … but not before Silver had picked up an ice cream, of course.

CHAPTER 6

It was all going to plan. The cats had:

🐾 Made it into the zoo. **TICK!**

🐾 Survived the reptile house. **BIG TICK!**

🐾 Not been killed and eaten by tigers.
BIGGER TICK!

🐾 And they knew where Brian was
heading. **MASSIVE TICK!**

🐾 Lastly, Silver had eaten an ice cream.
TICKETY TICK!

They made their way out of the zoo and down a steep slope towards the canal. The night air was freezing cold and the grass was crispy with frost under their paws, but getting warm was the last thing on their minds – they had a snake to catch!

Before too long, they came to the sewer entrance. Neither Toto nor Silver really fancied going down there – it sounded like it was smelly, dirty and wet. And ever since

they'd found out where Brian was heading, Catface had been as quiet as a dormouse.

'Listen, chaps,' Catface suddenly spoke up, looking nervous. 'There's something I've been meaning to tell you. We're about to enter a lair of rats. They'll be everywhere down there and they'll be scared of you, because you're cats. But not me ... because they know me ... because ... I'm from there, because ... I'm not exactly a cat, I'm more, how can I put it? Well. **I'M A RAT**.'

Toto stared, her mouth wide open. Silver did a backwards somersault. 'I knew it – I just knew it! You can't jump, you have funny teeth and you are way too weird for a cat. What happens now? Do we eat him?'

'No, we DO NOT eat him,' Toto said. 'Catface, what are you talking about?'

'Well, as you know my nickname is Catface. It was given to me by my family, but not in a nice way. It's because I look so much like a cat and no one knows why. My real name is Alexandre Rattinoff – Alexandre after the man who discovered the Black Plague. Which, by the way, wasn't our fault, it was those pesky fleas. And the surname is RATtinoff, see ...'

'*Riiiight*,' said Toto. 'But why do you

live your life as a cat?'

'It's very simple, and also a bit complicated. I am from rat royalty – you can trace my family back to 1665. They survived the Great Fire of London, and since then the Rattinoffs have ruled Rat London, along with five other rat families, and I am the rightful heir to the throne. Unfortunately, I was far from welcome in polite rat society. Imagine! The heir born looking like our sworn enemy. To my father I was a disgrace, so I started leaving the sewers and coming up here, and I realised that I quite liked it. No one thought I was a rat. I was treated as one of them – one of you! I got to hang around street corners, I learnt to do a pretty decent meow, and everyone seemed to like me, so eventually I just became …'

'A cat,' said Toto.

'Exactly,' said Catface. 'But when my father heard I was friends with the enemy, bringing shame on our good name, I was banished for good. And now I have to go down there and face him again. But there's a King Cobra on the loose, who just happens to *love* eating rats, and I do still love my family, so I guess I've got no choice. Are you still with me?'

'Of course we are,' said Toto. 'Until a couple of hours ago we didn't really know anyone in this town. Now we couldn't imagine living anywhere else. That's down to you! Rat or cat, you're our friend, Catface … or should we call you Alex?'

'Catface will do just fine,' grinned their new rat friend, whose teeth really did look quite rat-like when they thought about it.

'We won't let you down,' said Toto. 'Besides, who knew rats could be so charming! Right, Silver?'

'So just to be clear,' said Silver, 'we're not going to eat him?'

Catface looked pale.

'Joke!' said Silver. 'Of course, sis – Catface is the rat's whiskers!

←LONDON   RATBOROUGH→

Let's go into a lair of rats that hate us to find a
cobra who'll eat us ... it should be fun!'

So, taking one last look at the London
night, they took a deep breath and entered
the sewer.

'GET YOUR SCRAP BURGER HERE! GET THEM WHILE THEY'RE HOT!'

The yell of the rat market trader was the first thing the brave animal gang heard when they emerged in the central square of Ratborough – the capital of Rat London – which, for you and I, is about fifteen metres under Camden High Street.

They'd travelled through the dark, smelly sewers for what seemed like ages, trying to avoid bumping into any rats along the way. Luckily, as there were so many smaller tunnels leading off from the main one, which they could hide in when necessary, they had gone undetected. But as they got closer to the town, it became busier and busier, so Catface had pulled his hat right down and hidden the cats under his coat-tails.

After a while, the sewer tunnels got bigger and bigger, and they started to pass small rat houses made from mud and rubbish. The houses got larger and grander, until finally the tunnel opened on to the huge town square. In the middle was a vast park, surrounded by buildings made from plastic, glass bottles, tin cans and toilet rolls. A sewer river ran through it all, and just nearby the food market was in full swing.

'Catface, this place is incredible!' said Silver.

'Is this where you're from?' asked Toto.

'I was born and bred here – I grew up in the palace over there,' Catface said, pointing to a beautiful building made from glass cola bottles.

There were rats *everywhere*. Luckily, they were all too busy going about their business to notice the large rat, under a hat, who looked like a cat, and the two tails that stuck out from underneath his tweed jacket.

The smell from the food stalls was overwhelming – fried, dirty, slightly off meat.

Silver loved it. 'Now *this* is my kind of place! What's in a scrap burger anyway?'

'You do NOT want to know, my friend,' replied Catface. 'Let's just say, the clue is in the name.'

'So, what's the plan?' asked Toto, as they found a quieter corner to huddle in. 'We can't just start screaming, "There's a King

Cobra on the loose – run for the hills!" Are there even any hills here?'

'No, and no,' said Catface, glancing down. 'Oh, Silver, not again!'

Silver had slipped out from underneath Catface's coat-tails and was hiding in a bush next to the scrap burger stand. Just as his paw was about to nab one of the burgers, the stallholder turned and caught him in the act. At first the stallholder looked furious, then confused, then scared ...

'THIEF! CAT! CAT-THIEF!' he screamed.

Within seconds, from the four corners of the square ran ten uniformed rats armed with pikes (which looked suspiciously like toothpicks), who surrounded the cats.

'Sorry, sis – thought I'd get away with it ...'

said Silver sheepishly, backing away.

'Any ideas, Catface?' asked Toto.

'Alas, no,' he said. 'This is the King's Guard, the elite warriors of my father's army. I'm his son, and even I'm not sure I can talk us out of this one.'

'Right then,' said Toto. 'I've got this.'

She took a step back and closed her eyes. She could sense the guards were all big, strong and armed, but at least she knew exactly where they were. Drawing a breath, she emptied her mind and knew what to do.

As the first guard moved to attack, she dodged and leapt up in the air, avoiding the stabbing toothpick that was heading her way. She hung in the air for what seemed like an age, then swept her back foot around in a circle, swiping the surrounding rats in their faces with her spiky claws. By the time she landed half a second later, all ten rat guards were lying on the ground, groaning.

'CLASSIC NINJA MOVE!' said Silver, grinning. 'One of my favourites.'

Catface was staring open-mouthed, but

reinforcements were coming from all sides, and before they knew it, a hundred or so armed rats had surrounded them.

'She can take them all, just watch her!' said Silver excitedly.

'**ENOUGH!**' A booming voice echoed around the whole square.

All eyes turned towards the palace as the owner of the voice started to walk down the stairs towards them.

He was enormous, dressed in fine robes, with a ridiculous, old-fashioned hat. He also looked quite a lot like a cat.

'Let me guess,' said Toto. 'Your dad?'

'Yes, he's the king all right,' said Catface. 'Whatever you do, do NOT say that we look like each other.'

'But you look exactly like each other,' protested Silver.

'NOT A WORD,' said Catface. 'Let me see if I can handle this. Wish me luck.'

Catface took off his hat and walked towards his dad. The guards gave way, suddenly realising who he was.

'YOU!' The king sounded furious. 'Who gave you permission to return here? You have been banished to live with the surface dwellers you love so much. I know for a fact that you are still seen in the company of cats – **CATS!**'

The whole town square took a massive gasp as one.

'And now I see you return with two *cat assassins* to overthrow me and claim the crown for yourself!'

'You know, that's not a bad idea,' whispered Silver to Toto.

'Father!' said Catface. 'I've done no such

thing. I'm here to help you. It is true, I am a surface dweller – which is a weird thing to call them, by the way – but there are many creatures up there who wish us no harm.'

Silver whistled and looked away.

'These are my friends,' Catface continued, gesturing to Silver and Toto, 'and we come with a warning. You have to listen to us. A King Cobra, *the* King Cobra – the terrifying monster known only as Brian – has escaped from the zoo, and could be heading this way!'

'Pah!' said the king. 'We already know! Our scouts warned us that he was spotted in one of the nearby tunnels. Ten of my finest men and I were about to go and capture him.' The king glanced over at the armed rats lying on the ground. 'Argh, what have you done? They were my best warriors!'

'Ah. Sorry about that. Yes, that might have been us,' said Catface.

Catface's dad looked uneasy, but he couldn't back down with the whole town watching.

'I see ... er ... no matter!' he said nervously. 'I shall go with the rest of my men and capture Brian. I trained these warriors personally, and I have fought other snakes in my time. Brian poses no threat to our skills.'

A couple of the rats in the King's Guard looked doubtfully at each other.

'Do you remember him training us?' one whispered.

'I remember him eating cakes and *watching* us train. I'm not sure that's the same thing,' his friend whispered back.

PSSSTT
PSSSTT

'And you, my so-called son,' continued the king, 'and you two cats who have come here to overthrow me – you shall come with me, so you can bear witness that I, Henrich Rattinoff, 835th of my name, King of Camden, Regent's Park, Primrose Hill, and the outlying boroughs that I occasionally visit, twinned incidentally with Frederiksberg, Luxembourg, and Mochudi in Botswana, am the true leader of these people and that no snake can beat me. Guards! Seize them!'

'This guy has serious issues,' Toto whispered to Silver, as they were surrounded by even more rat guards. 'Should I take them out?'

Catface shook his head. 'I don't think so, little one – you can't take on a hundred rats and, to be frank, I think the only thing that can save my father from Brian is if we go along for the ride ...'

For the first time, Toto felt scared. Had she finally bitten off more than a ninja cat should?

CHAPTER 7

It seemed as if they'd been walking through the sewers for ever. They'd left Ratborough far behind and were following the canal towards the tunnel where Brian had been spotted by the rat scouts.

Toto, Silver and Catface were bound in pawcuffs (which looked a lot like pink gift ribbon). Toto could see the shadows cast by the guards' torches (which looked a lot like lit matches), turning them all into giants. *We'll need to fight like giants if we're going to stand any chance against Brian*, she thought to herself.

Up ahead, Catface's dad was being carried along by some less-than-happy rat soldiers on a throne constructed from an old flannel and a pincushion, held together by toothbrushes and twigs. At the front of the procession, a rat scout scurried about, sniffing here and there.

'I'm getting close,' he yelled. The rats all shouted words of encouragement as they held their torches aloft.

'Well, my son, let's see how my army and I deal with this monster of yours,' the king shouted over to Catface. 'HALT!' The hundred-strong army came to a standstill.

'Bring the prisoners up here!' cried the king, just as the rat scout returned from a tunnel up ahead. He looked petrified.

'Th-th-the snake ... he's up there, through that tunnel! It comes out into a small chamber with a pool. He's resting on the bank at the side. I don't think he saw me, but ... he's awfully big – massive fangs, clever eyes, huge tail – you'd be *mad* to ...' He petered off as he saw the king glaring at him. 'I'm sure he's no match for your army, my king,' he finished, bowing low.

The king gave him a look of disgust, then turned to his general.

'OK, my loyal subject, here's the plan,' the king said, sounding confident. 'All one hundred of us will rush through the tunnel, surrounding Brian on all sides. I'll stab him in the tail – you go for the head and subdue the beast. Yes, that sounds fair. Deal?'

The general looked as if he thought that was a terrible idea, but he saluted anyhow.

'Right,' the king addressed his troops. 'Today is the day we show all those surface dwellers that we rats rule this city, and that we can defeat this monster called Brian. If you love your town and your family, follow me!'

Toto, Silver and Catface were dragged along by the force of the crowd, and before they knew it they were out of the tunnel and into the chamber, facing the bank opposite. There, curled up in a massive coil of green and olive scales, was an enormous snake. He looked ferocious; he looked terrifying; he looked … asleep.

'Well, that was a bit of an anticlimax,' said Silver.

Slowly, the army of rats edged its way towards the sleeping snake, with lit matches and toothpicks held aloft.

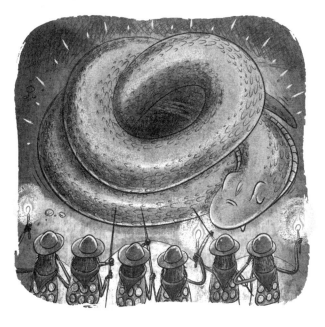

But Toto wasn't fooled. She knew this was the most deadly predator she'd ever faced.

She'd seen grass snakes before, back in Italy. They often looked as if they were sleeping, but they could spring to life at any moment.

'This is going to end badly,' Toto whispered to Catface and Silver. 'We need to get out of these pawcuffs.'

'SEE!' boomed the king. 'I told you I'd capture it. Hardly a monster after all, but a big sleeping—'

A scream from all the rats in unison cut through the air, and as the king turned he saw his whole army fleeing back through the tunnel.

And the reason? Brian had woken up – and he wasn't overly happy with his morning view of an army of rats ready to attack him.

So he did what any self-respecting King Cobra would do – he reared up and started to spread his hood, which would be a terrifying sight for anyone, but especially when you are his chosen prey.

'I hate to say I told you so,' said Toto, desperately scrabbling at her pawcuffs.

Their guards had long since scarpered, leaving the king, Catface, Toto and Silver to face Brian alone.

'Catface, quickly, gnaw through the pawcuffs!' said Toto.

'On it,' said Catface. His big teeth went to work and in a jiffy they were all free.

'It is amazing,' said Silver, as they ran over to Catface's dad, 'that we didn't spot that he was a rat sooner. Those gnashers!'

'Not the right time, bro,' said Toto.

They stopped halfway into the pool of water. The snake had fully spread his hood and was standing two metres in the air.

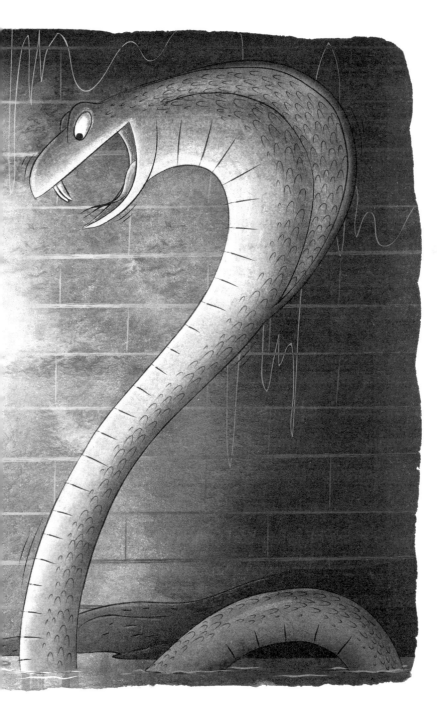

He was nearly touching the ceiling of the sewer and making a terrible noise, almost growling. In front of the cobra stood Catface's dad, armed only with a toothpick.

'RUN!' the king turned and shouted at Catface. **'GET OUT OF HERE, SON!'**

'No, Father, wait, I'm coming,' Catface yelled, as he ran towards his dad.

The giant snake rolled his eyes, and with a swish of his powerful tail he sent Catface and his dad crashing into a wall. They fell unconscious in a heap.

'That went well! You're up, sis. Be careful,' added Silver.

Although he sounded confident, Toto could tell Silver was scared for her.

Toto knew she'd never come up against

anything like this before. An army of rats was one thing, or the neighbourhood cats back in Italy who had tried to bully her and Silver; even the tigers with their massive teeth seemed easier than what she was facing now – one of the deadliest snakes in the world. Despite all of her training from her master back in Italy, Brian could still crush her, he could bite her in two, or he could sink his fangs in and let his lethal venom do the job.

Great, so many wonderful ways to die, she thought to herself. *Think happy thoughts, Toto, think happy thoughts.*

'Watch out for those fangs, sis,' said Silver. 'They look deadly.'

'Thanks, Silver. Helpful. I'll bear that in mind,' said Toto.

The light was dim, which meant what little eyesight Toto had was next to useless. What she could *hear*, however, was Brian moving through the water towards her, getting closer and closer and ready to strike; she sensed him arch his muscly body, and felt the water ripple around

her. Suddenly, he launched himself at Toto, but as he was about to sink his fangs into her she leapt out of the way ... just in the nick of time.

CRUNCH

MAMMA MIA! *This guy is fast!* Toto thought to herself. She was scared.

Right, she thought. *He's more powerful than me, he's more deadly than me and he's as fast as me. I'm not sure I can get close enough to lay a paw on him ... the only thing to do is tire this guy out before I'm done for.*

And so, every time the snake had Toto in range of his deadly fangs, she leapt out of the way just before he could bite her. It was so much harder than her battle with Jae Jae. There were no branches to jump to, and Brian's strike was lightning fast.

Toto knew she couldn't keep it up – she too was getting tired and she was running out of ideas. She had her back to the wall of the chamber near where the water flowed into the pool. As Brian charged once more, she dodged out of the way, just in time to see him bounce off the side of the wall, loosening a few bricks. **THIS WAS HER CHANCE!** If she could get Brian to strike at the right point of the wall, with a little push the whole thing would come down on him, giving him one almighty headache.

Toto knew she'd only get one shot at it. After that, her stamina would wear too thin, and she'd surely be caught in Brian's fangs.

Brian moved to strike one more time, arching his great back, his hood flared and eyes alert.

Toto shut her eyes, took a deep breath, remembered her training and trusted her instincts. She felt the air rushing towards her. Knowing the snake was centimetres away, she jumped, hung in the air to dodge Brian's lunge, then spun her body around and landed on Brian's head!

Hurtling through the night air, she put her paws behind his neck and threw him into the wall, jumping off at the last second. She landed with an effortless roll and turned to see the wall give way. It came crashing down around the snake, trapping the middle section of his body.

Brian was furious! He let out a terrifying hiss, just before one last brick hit him on the head and knocked him out cold.

Catface and his father stirred at the sound.

Silver ran to Toto. 'That was incredible! Your best fight ever. Talk us through it. Were you toying with him? You were, weren't you?'

'Oh, brother, no post-fight interview now,' said Toto. 'I'm shattered. Let's just get Brian back to the zoo, then we can head home. Speaking of which ... Er, how exactly do we carry a King Cobra back to the zoo?'

Silver was prodding the snake with a toothpick. 'He's still breathing, so—'

He was interrupted by a loud groan. It was Brian!

'*OWWWW.* My head is killing me! What's the matter with you people? First rats, then cats ... Why don't you leave me alone?'

'Leave you alone?' said Toto. 'You've escaped the zoo to feast on the animals of London. Of course we're going to stop you!'

'Feast on the animals of London? What are you talking about? Did I attack you first? No! Did any of you bother to ask before you formed this angry mob to hunt me down? Listen, I ate last week and I'm not due another feed for weeks, maybe months. So yes, you all look very tasty, especially that

portly gentleman over there –' he nodded to the king, who looked behind him as if Brian were talking about someone totally different – 'but I'm not hungry. So WHY are you hunting me?'

All the cats and rats looked down at the ground, a little ashamed and very embarrassed.

'*THIS IS AWKWARD*,' said Silver.

'Er ...' said Catface. 'We heard you had escaped from the zoo and ... naturally, you know, feared the worst ... You're Brian the King Cobra – your name is famous throughout the land. Everyone outside the zoo is terrified of you.'

'Really?' said Brian, sounding shocked. 'I mean, I know I might look a bit scary, but I'm quite friendly really. I get on like a house on fire with Julio the pit viper from next door.'

'Hmm. So why have you escaped?' asked Toto.

'My girlfriend,' said Brian.

'Excuse me?' they all said together.

'Yep, her name is Brenda. We've known each other since we were eggs, but we got separated a year ago. I thought I'd lost her.

But last week a new western diamondback rattlesnake called Eric turns up after being rescued from some illegal pet dealers, saying he's seen her in a flat in St John's Wood. So I'm off to save her – at least I was until you *put a wall on my head* …'

'Right, so, you'll just get her and go back to the zoo?' asked Silver. 'Without, you know, *eating* anyone?'

'Of course! It's my home, all my friends are there, the climate's great, and the food's fantastic and much easier than hunting the likes of you lot. I just want to rescue my girlfriend. I've got the address, but I'm a massive snake, so I'm hardly inconspicuous. Plus, I've got no fingers or thumbs, so I'm not sure how I'll get in and how I'll get her out!'

The cats and rats all looked at each other.

Toto knew exactly what had to be done. 'Well, that's where we can help. Get us there and we'll do the rest,' she said. 'After what we've put you through, it's the least we can do.'

'Really?' said Brian. 'Thank you!'

They all smiled at Brian for a moment, then stood awkwardly, as if they weren't sure what to do next.

'Er,' piped up Brian, 'I don't suppose you could get this wall off me so we can get going?'

'Oh yes, sorry!' said Toto.

'Quite all right,' said Brian, as they cleared the rubble from around him. 'You are a very good fighter, little cat – my head is going to hurt for a week! Right, cats, rats and whatever you are,' he said, nodding to Catface, **'*HOP ON, WE'VE GOT A SNAKE TO RESCUE!*'**

CHAPTER 8

The rats who lived in the sewers on the way to St John's Wood looked on in awe as their king, his banished son and two cats slithered by at great speed ... on the back of a giant snake.

'I imagine I'll have some explaining to do when I get back to Ratborough!' the king said, as he waved to his confused subjects. 'The papers will have a field day. Still, it takes me back to the old days – I used these tunnels to escape after the Great Cheese Heist. Happy times! Ah, we're nearly here. Take the next left, then after ten or so metres there should be a ladder to the nearest drain.'

Sure enough, the king's directions were spot on, and they reached St John's Wood in no time. Under the cover of darkness, the rather odd-looking party of two cats, two rats and a snake made their way out of a drain and into the shrubbery that bordered a block of flats. Brenda was apparently being held on the second floor.

'OK, here's the plan,' said Toto. 'Silver and I will scale the wall. We'll scope the place to see if Brenda's there, then call down to you guys. Er … she won't try to eat us, will she?'

'Good point,' said Brian. 'Maybe I should come with you.'

'You can climb?' asked Silver.

'Of course, I just don't have paws, or claws, or fingers, or thumbs … but other than that …' He shrugged, or he would have done, but he didn't have any shoulders.

Toto and Silver started their climb. Brian wrapped himself around a drainpipe and slithered up.

Before too long they'd reached a window ledge on the second floor.

'This should be it,' said Brian, peering in.

They could see they were in the right place. Silver described the scene to Toto. The front room was full of row upon row of tanks containing lizards, frogs and snakes,

and at the very end was a big snake just like Brian, fast asleep.

'There she is. Isn't she a beauty?' sighed Brian.

Silver gulped. 'Not sure I fancy going in there, sis,' he said. 'I think we might look a bit too much like breakfast.'

'We have no choice,' said Toto. She looked up and could just about make out that the top window was open. 'Look, I'll try to make it in through there, and I'll open the bottom window from the other side. Then, Brian, you go and wake Brenda up, tell her not to eat us, and we'll all get out of here. Sound like a plan?'

Silver put two paws up, while Brian smiled a big, goofy, lovestruck grin, his forked tongue hanging to one side.

'Weird,' said Toto, 'but I think that's a yes.'

Toto climbed stealthily to the window, scrambled through and dropped silently down into the room. She couldn't see much, but the sky outside was getting brighter, which gave her just enough light to make out some shapes. So far, all was going to plan, she just had to get the bottom window open and ...

A light went on in the hall, and she could hear footsteps.

'Someone's coming! Hide!' she whispered to Brian and Silver. They ducked out of the way, but Toto was stranded. Quickly, she ninja-chopped the padlock of the first tank she got to, and scrambled inside, just as a man with a clipboard walked in.

'Ernie!' the man called to someone outside the room. 'We've got fifty of these rare ones to be shipped in an hour, all in the back of the van. The usual drop-off to avoid the police. I'm just checking on the snakes and spiders, then we can start moving.'

They must be the illegal pet dealers Brian heard about! Toto thought. *I've got to move fast! If I can just get to the tank where Brenda ... hang on, what did he mean, spiders?*

Slowly, Toto turned towards the back of the tank.

A big black furry ball started to unravel, gradually extending its legs, until in front of Toto was the **BIGGEST SPIDER** she'd ever encountered.

As bad situations go, this was up there. Toto might have fought tigers and an enormous snake in the last couple of hours, but this was a tight spot, and she couldn't use any of her ninja moves while trapped in such a small tank.

The spider began creeping towards her. Toto glanced at the man, checking the tanks and cages as he made his way through the room. There was nowhere to hide! Toto shrank back and got ready to draw her claws, when suddenly the man appeared at the spider's cage.

He looked at the spider, then at Toto, a look of pure bewilderment on his face.

'ERNIE! We've got a cat in here!' he shouted.

This was the chance Toto needed. She sprang out of the tank, hitting the man square in the face and knocking him over. Thinking quickly, she bounced off his head and leapt for Brenda's tank, then ninja-chopped her lock too.

The cobra woke up and immediately sprang for Toto. 'Breakfast!' Brenda hissed.

Toto jumped as high as she could, clinging with one paw to the ceiling light.

'Not quite,' Toto called down. 'I'm here on a mission to rescue you. I'm with Brian ...' She gestured to the window, where Brian was smiling back like a lovesick puppy.

'*MY HONEYBUN!*' Brenda cooed.

Silver laughed so hard he almost fell

off the window ledge.

'I know you might think this is a bit weird, a cat coming to your rescue,' said Toto, 'but go with it, and please don't try to eat me.'

'Got it,' replied the snake.

Toto dropped down and they raced over to the window. Toto managed to open it and they tumbled on to the ledge.

'OH, MY MUNCHKIN!' cried Brian.

'MY BRIANY-WINY!' said Brenda, as they wound around each other.

'I hate to break this up, but we need to leave – *now*,' said Silver.

'We can't go without rescuing the others!' said Brenda.

'Have you lost your mind?' asked Silver. 'You want us to release a whole animal-eating army?'

'Oh, I'm the only one you have to worry about,' said Brenda. 'The rest of them just eat insects and worms, and the occasional rat ...'

'Er ... best not mention that,' said Silver.

'But if we leave them here they'll be sold off and taken to who knows where and they'll never see their families again,' said Brenda.

'OK,' said Toto, 'leave it to me. You guys get going – I'll be right behind you.'

Silver and the snakes started climbing down the drainpipe to freedom.

Toto unsheathed her claws, and in four quick ninja-chops she'd broken into the tanks.

BAM

'Here, you pesky moggy!' The man had come around, and he sounded angry!

Toto needed to get back to the window, and fast. She made one almighty jump on to the man's head and pushed his cap down over his eyes, then sprang up once more and reached the ledge.

A procession of lizards, frogs, spiders and iguanas came scuttling out of their tanks, on to the man.

'Argh! Spiders! Lizards! Argh! I'm getting out of here. Ernie!'

'Best of luck, you lot,' Toto called to the escaped animals, 'and please don't eat any rats – they're not a bad bunch, you know.'

And Toto the ninja cat leapt out into the cold night air.

CHAPTER 9

It was the strangest day in Ratborough's history. The good rats of the town were just a bit confused. On the balcony of the palace, their king was parading his son – who was supposed to be banished – plus two cats and two snakes, as heroes!

It was Brian of all people, or of all snakes, who had suggested it in the sewers on the way home.

'Your Highness,' he'd said to the king, who was riding on his back through the tunnels, 'when we get to Ratborough, it might look a little odd to your folk that we're now friends, seeing as the last they heard you were about to take me on with a toothpick. I just wouldn't want you to look ... well ... silly. Unkingly. Weak. Dare I say, *an idiot*—'

'Yes, yes, I see,' interrupted the king, 'that

SWOOOSH

is a good point. What do you suggest we say?'

'How about that you, your son and I fought, and that you two were so good, I admitted defeat. And then in my exhausted state you took mercy on me and, together with the cats, helped me rescue my true love, thus cementing an eternal friendship between rats and snakes ... *TA-DA!*'

'I like it, and it's almost the truth,' said the king.

'Apart from the quite important bit about you and Catface *not* defeating him,' said Silver. 'I seem to remember you lasted approximately ten seconds—'

'Yes, yes, well, we can gloss over that ... What they won't know won't hurt them!' said the king.

'What about me, Father?' said Catface. 'Am I welcome home?'

'After all we've been through tonight, my boy, I've never been more proud of you. I'm sorry for everything. I was just jealous of you, at home up there on the streets, with all those surface dwellers. Tell me, are cats as cool as they look?'

'Father,' Catface said, smiling at Toto and Silver, 'cool doesn't even come close.'

The town square had been decked out in all its ratty finery, and was filled with rats cheering and dancing and waving flags with the Rattinoff coat of arms.

Rat trumpeters were tooting a jaunty tune, while little rats played games in the park surrounded by delicious-smelling food stalls.

'You have to hand it to rats,' said Silver to Toto, as they gazed over the scene from the balcony of the cola bottle palace, 'they know how throw a party ... I HAVE to get myself one of those scrap burgers before we leave.'

'Today marks a brave new day in the history of rats, cats and snakes,' proclaimed the king to his people. 'From this day forth, we are no longer enemies, and our friends Brian and Brenda are awarded the keys to the city!'

'Not your father's brightest idea,' whispered Brian to Catface. 'I've gone right off rats, but Brenda loves them. She won't need feeding for a while, but I wouldn't exactly invite her to visit!'

'Right,' said Catface, looking pale. 'I'll ... er ... mention it to Father later.'

'And for the mighty Toto and her brother, Silver,' continued the king, 'we accord them the highest honour in the kingdom of the rats: **_THE CROWN OF CHEESE!_**'

A couple of the King's Guard brought out a crown made of really stinky cheese – a combination of Camembert, Stilton and Red Leicester, from what Toto could smell.

'WHAT?' whispered Toto. 'I'm not wearing that!'

'You have to!' said Catface. 'It's the greatest honour in our kingdom. It means you go down in history as a friend of the rats.'

'And that you look like a muppet!' said Silver, chuckling.

'I don't know what you're laughing at,' said Toto. 'There's one for you too!'

'WHAT?'

They could only stand there as they were both adorned with their crowns and the town applauded, while they felt ... well ... a little bit silly ... and *very* smelly.

'And lastly,' said the king, 'to my son, Catface. Yes, he may look like one of our sworn enemies, the cats—'

'Hey!' exclaimed Toto and Silver.

'I mean, our *old* enemies, the cats,' corrected the king, 'but the bravery Catface showed today in saving me and, indeed, the whole town from Brian the King Cobra was nothing short of heroic ...'

'Laying it on a bit thick, isn't he?' hissed Brian.

'Catface, or Alex – as your mother and I named you,' said the king, 'you are the rightful heir of Ratborough, and you are welcome back any time.'

'Thank you, Father,' said Catface, hugging his dad. 'I think I'll stay topside for now though. Like you said, cats are cool!'

'AND NOW,' proclaimed the king, **'LET US PARTY LIKE RATS ON A HOT TIN ROOF.**

CHEESE ALL ROUND!'

The town square erupted with cheers and clapping. The music and dancing started up again, with rat-sized violins, accordions and flutes playing the latest rat hits. It was going to be one big party!

'Brian, I'd like to thank you for everything,' the king said, turning to him.

Brian smiled his goofy grin. 'No problem at all. Thanks for helping me rescue my one true love! And listen, if you ever have any trouble with bigger rats from out of town, you know who to call. We can take care of them, if you know what I mean,' said Brian with a wink.

'Er, thanks for the offer,' the king said, looking a bit flustered.

'Well, you know where we are,' said Brian. 'See you soon!'

With a nod of thanks to the cats, the two snakes slithered off, tails entwined, back towards the zoo.

Meanwhile, yellow cheesy stuff was flying from all of the food stalls. 'This is going to get messy,' said Catface, leading Toto and Silver from the balcony. 'Let's get you home before the sun comes up.'

'I could sleep for a week,' said Silver. 'Let's go.'

'No argument here,' said Toto, yawning. 'Tell me, when is it *not* considered rude to take these cheese helmets off?!'

CHAPTER 10

The early morning sun was turning the sky a cold but beautiful orange as Catface walked the cats back to their house. They were so exhausted that even with her ninja training Toto struggled to get over the gate.

They poked their heads through the bars to say goodbye to Catface.

'Well, my little ones,' Catface said, 'that

was quite enough of an adventure for one night. I for one am tuckered out, but I'm so glad you caught me putting my snout in your bins. I want to thank you. I'm back with my father, and my people, and most importantly I'm proud of who I am: Catface the rat, who looks like a cat. It's all thanks to you two, my little warrior cats from Italy. And you, young lady –' he gestured a paw to Toto – 'must teach me some of those ninja moves!'

'I will!' said Toto. 'We'd heard London was a hectic town, but we hadn't expected it to be as crazy as this! Can we take a couple of nights off before we do it again?!'

Catface smiled. 'Of course ... see you both soon.' He gave them a wink, tipped his hat, and headed off with a carefree walk into the dawn air, whistling as he went.

The cats almost fell through the cat flap. They went straight to the kitchen, where they demolished the bowls of food left over from the night before, then padded upstairs to bed, where their parents were beginning to stir from a good night's sleep.

'You missing Italy any more, sis?' Silver said as they jumped up on to the foot of the bed.

'A bit, but you know, I think we'll fit in here just fine.'

'Me too,' said Silver. 'Night, sis ...'

'Night, bro.'

They fell fast asleep, curled up together, just as their parents' morning alarm went off and the lights flicked on.

'Come on, you two, up for breakfast,' said Mamma. 'Toto, Silver, wakey-wakey ...'

'We have the laziest cats in the world!' said Papa.

But neither cat heard. They were already dreaming about the craziest night of their short lives ...

Back at London Zoo, the night keepers were doing their last rounds. It had been a weird night. The animals had been making loads of noise for hours, but thankfully it was nearly the end of the keepers' shift.

'Come on, Derek, let's head back. I'm starving,' Norman said to his friend. He was looking forward to a nice fry up with lots of hot sweet tea.

'I'll be right with you, Norman. Just going to do one last check on the reptile house.'

'Right you are, well, get a move on.'

Derek opened the heavy oak doors, and

walked slowly around the reptile house, careful to keep his torchlight down so as not to wake up any of the animals.

As he walked past the last tank he glanced inside, looked away, then did a double take. He rubbed his eyes and got on his walkie-talkie.

'ER ... NORMAN ... HOW MANY KING COBRAS ARE WE SUPPOSED TO HAVE?'

THE END

ACKNOWLEDGEMENTS

Firstly, thank you to my (very) patient, understanding, smart, inventive, supportive team at Hachette.

Special thanks to Anne McNeil, Alison Padley, and big love to the tireless Sarah Lambert (you should have been a Marine) for hearing my pitch (a 'true' story about my actual blind ninja cat), then having the faith and trust in a first time novelist to let me realise it.

Thanks to the incredible talent, excellent lunch companion, and the all round good guy that is Nick East. I've loved watching you bring Toto, Silver, Catface, all the characters and dear old London town to life, in such a vivid way, and thanks for being so considerate and understanding with me and my rudimentary grasp of the world of illustration.

To my team at John Noel Management: John, Jonny and Jess, who stoically and doggedly steer the ship, wherever I may choose to point it, without complaint or hesitation, and always with good grace and unconditional support.

To Liz, Jordan, the sorely missed force of nature that was Sophie and all at LMPR for their hard work, smarts, and all round outstanding glam squad game.

To my niece, Josette. By far the brightest star in the O'Leary clan (yes, I know 'You're a Stick as well as an O'Leary'), whose love of reading and all things books is a credit to her parents, grandparents and her uncle.

To all the team at The Village Vets of Belsize Park, especially to Fran, Kate, Chantelle, Helen, Victoria, Debbie and Adam, for looking after our Silver boy and giving him seven extra glorious months.

Thanks to my wife Dee (always) for the hours of effort and inspiration, and helping me shape our little cats on paper, turning them into the heroes we know they are.

And lastly, thanks to the stars of the show, Toto and Silver themselves. Thanks for coming into our lives, as just two little Italian strays, and choosing to make us your mamma and papa. Silver, you'll always be our little rock star, and Toto, I'm sorry to blow your cover, but your story is too incredible not to be told. Thanks for being our little ninja.

AUTHOR Q AND A
MEET DERMOT!

Hi Dermot! Your book is all about your real-life cats. Can you tell us more about them?

We have a little place in Italy in the middle of nowhere, in Puglia. It's wild countryside and when we first got there we had a lot of rats. Then this cat took up residence – we called her Plaxy after one of the guests – and she was more stray than feral so you could stroke her, but you couldn't really pick her up. But as time went on, she got more tame and ended up sleeping on our bed, which we loved. Then we went back about four years ago and Plaxy was heavily pregnant. I had to come back a day early for work but my wife Dee FaceTimed me to tell me Plaxy was having her kittens right there and then – in our room, and specifically in my pillowcase!

We were going to get a dog that year but then we had these four kittens and Dee had stayed up all night, doing this deft piece of cat midwifery. So we took two of the kittens and our neighbours took the other two. We had the firstborn, Silver, and Toto, the runt of the litter. Our friends looked after them out there in Italy and eventually we brought them to the UK.

Did you have pets when you were a kid?

No cats, but we had a rabbit growing up, and I was devastated when it died. The greatest moment of treachery in my whole life was when my mum and dad moved house from the village I grew up in and they said I could have a dog. Then as soon as they moved they said no. Oh it was awful!

Did you enjoy reading when you were younger?

Oh yes, and I remember the joy of page-turning and the dialogue from Roald Dahl's books – *Fantastic Mr Fox* was always my favourite.

We love Brian the King Cobra's escape from London Zoo! Did you visit the snake house there?

I go to London Zoo all the time. The great thing about living round the corner is that whenever nieces and godkids and cousins come to stay, it's a really good day out on your doorstep!

Like the hero of the story, Toto is blind in real life, isn't she?

We worked out quite quickly that Toto couldn't really see that well. We took her to the vet and found she had no red blood cells in her eyes. They told us the camera is there, but there's no film in it, so she can see breaks in light but not much else.

We noticed really quickly, though, that Toto had lightning-fast reactions; if you were playing around she could just lash out with her claws, super swift. I thought this would make a lovely idea for a book: that one cat is a mild-mannered kitten during the day – and then a ninja by night!

Dermot was interviewed by Damian Kelleher

TOTO'S NINJA WORDSEARCH!

Can you find all the words in Toto's wordsearch?
They can be forwards, backwards, up, down and
diagonal. GOOD LUCK, NINJAS!

TOTO'S TIP:

Photocopy the page if you
don't want to write in your book!

I	K	A	J	N	I	N	T	T	G
C	O	B	R	A	E	Ż	Y	C	Y
S	A	X	T	S	L	S	L	L	E
T	A	P	E	E	J	T	A	E	R
L	U	T	T	C	R	P	T	V	C
Ż	U	U	S	H	A	O	I	H	H
O	M	B	X	A	T	F	E	I	A
O	H	E	W	O	P	E	T	P	N
G	V	M	T	D	S	Q	L	A	D
Q	C	V	R	E	V	L	I	S	C

TOTO
SILVER
CATFACE
TUBE
COBRA

NINJA
ZOO
CHEESE
ITALY
PASTA

DERMOT O'LEARY'S

television and radio work has made
him a household name.

Dermot started his career on T4 for Channel 4,
and went on to present and produce Big Brother's Little
Brother. In 2007 Dermot landed the coveted role hosting
ITV 1's The X Factor and presented eight consecutive
series, deftly holding the judges to account on a weekly
basis. Dermot has also chaired the debate, and interviewed
party leaders, for First Time Voters Question Time on
BBC3. He regularly presents Unicef's SoccerAid, and is also
the host of the National Television Awards.

This is all alongside hosting his own multi
award-winning BBC Radio 2 show every Saturday
(winner of three Sony Radio Awards), known for
its solid support of new and emerging bands.

In 2014 Dermot hosted the ground-breaking 'Live from
Space' season on Channel 4, which culminated in a major
interactive TV event featuring a live two-hour broadcast
from the International Space Station (ISS) and Mission
Control in Houston as the ISS completed an entire orbit
of the Earth. Later that year, Dermot's first book, *The
Soundtrack to My Life*, a musical memoir, was published by
Hodder, and is currently out in paperback.

Dermot made a much anticipated and triumphant return to
The X Factor in 2016.

Toto the Ninja Cat and the Great Snake Escape is
Dermot's first book for children.
He lives in London with his wife, Dee.